WELCOME TO THE
FRONT-OF-THE-BOOK
NATURE RESERVE

For Tess and David.

OXFORD
UNIVERSITY PRESS

Great Clarendon Street, Oxford OX2 6DP

Oxford University Press is a department of the University of Oxford.
It furthers the University's objective of excellence in research, scholarship,
and education by publishing worldwide

Oxford is a registered trade mark of Oxford University Press
in the UK and in certain other countries

First published in 2017
First published in paperback in 2018

British Library Cataloguing in Publication Data
Data available

ISBN: 978-0-19-274974-1 (paperback)

10 9 8 7 6 5 4 3 2 1

Printed in China

Paper used in the production of this book is a natural, recyclable product
made from wood grown in sustainable forests. The manufacturing process
conforms to the environmental regulations of the country of origin.

Visit www.richardbyrne.co.uk

I want to go first!
Richard BYRNE
TO THE BACK-OF-THE-BOOK WATERING HOLE
OXFORD
UNIVERSITY PRESS

The elephants were getting ready for the long march to the watering hole at the back of the book.

ELIZABETH ELEANOR ELTON

'Can I go first this time?'

'Sorry, Elphie

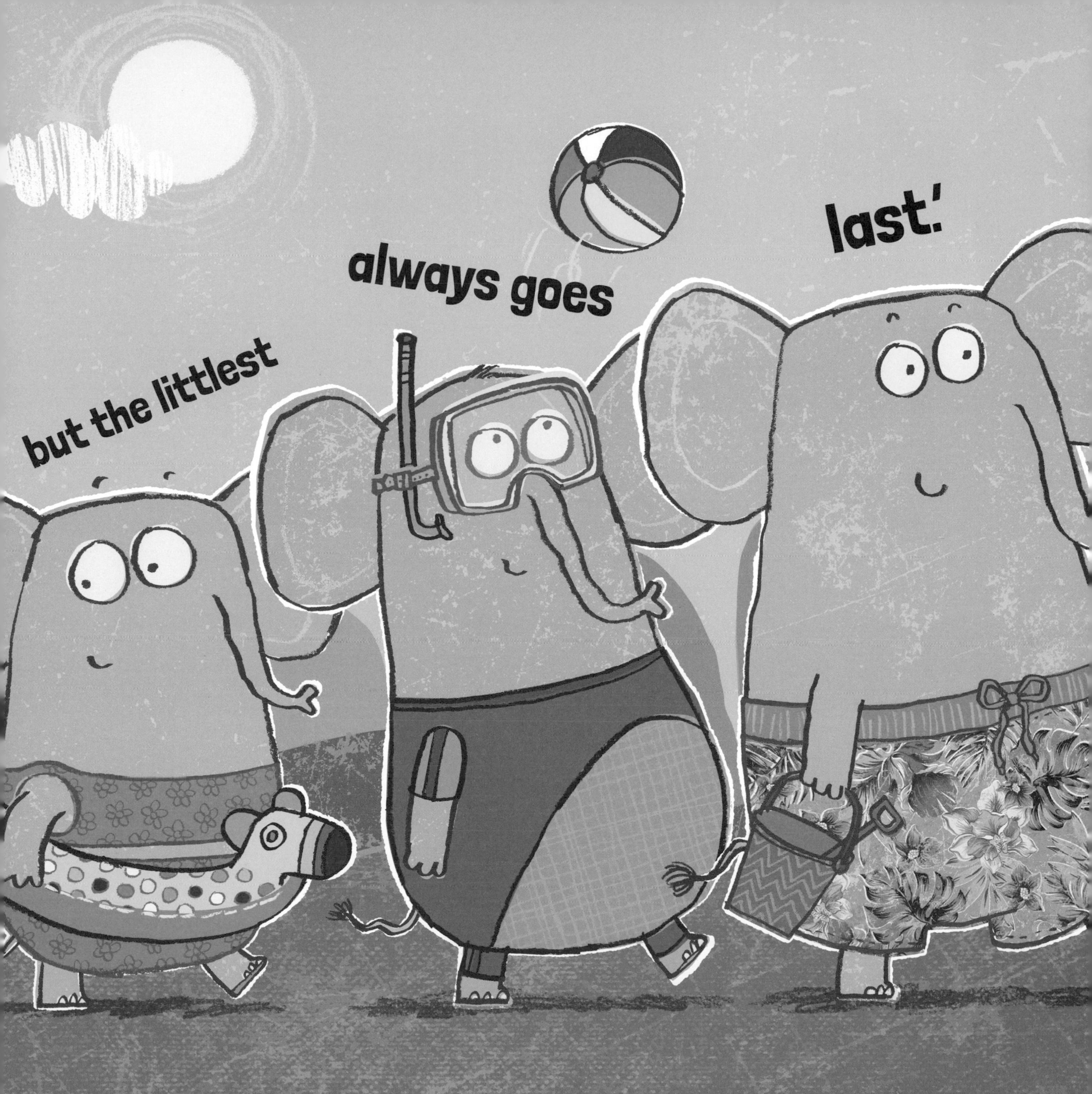
but the littlest
always goes
last.'

'But I really wanted to go first.'

'Think, think, think.'

Hey readers, I have an idea. On the count of three, shout out

ELEANOR!

Ready?
1... 2... 3...

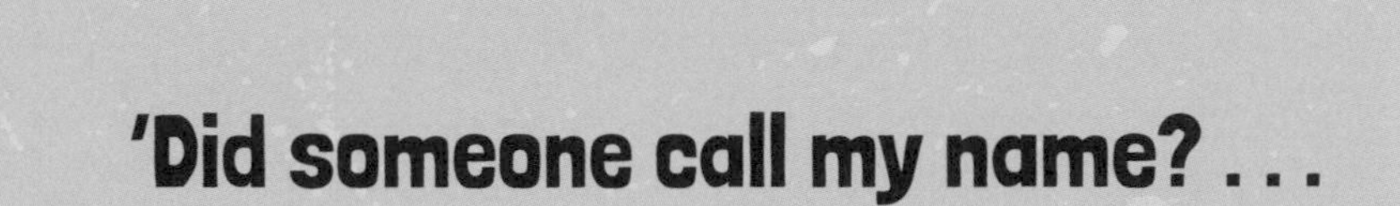

'Did someone call my name? . . .

You go on, Elphie.
I'd better wait here
to see who it is.'

Thank you readers. I'm not last any more!

'Hey, nobody turned up!
Wait for me!'

Now, can you make a loud hissing noise?

'Yikes, I can hear a

ssssnake!

I'll wait here for a while.
You go ahead, Elphie.'

'I'm back!
I think the snake has gone.'

Yippee! I'm in the middle.

This time please give the book a good wobble.

'After you. I'm not going on that bridge while it's so wobbly!'

'Look, I've made it across!
The bridge suddenly stopped wobbling!'

Hooray! Just one
more place to go.

This time can you
make a squeak-squeak
noise please?

It's not working.
Try growling!
Try snap-snapping!
TRY RRRRR

'Elgar, **STOP!** Didn't you hear the scary mouse? Or the frightening gorilla or crocodile or lion?'

'Don't be silly, Elphie. I'm not scared of noisy . . .

. . . readers!'
Uh-oh! We've been found out.

'Okay, we're here so let's all get
back into the right order, please.'
WELCOME TO THE
BACK-OF-THE-BOOK
WATERING
HOLE

'Oh dear, it looks like the watering hole is occupied.'

'Humph!'

'Yes it is! And I'm going to be here for a very, very long time so if I were you I'd come back on another day!'

Well he's a bit selfish, isn't he?
Can you do one last
extra loud
squeak-squeak please!

'Arghhhhh! I can hear a mouse!
I'm out of here!'

'Well done, Elphie!
We all think that when it's time
for the long march home . . .
Thank you readers.

. . . the cleverest
should
go
first!'